THE GHOST AT CODLIN CASTLE

Dick King-Smith is one of today's foremost writers for children. After serving in the Grenadier Guards during World War II, he farmed in Gloucestershire for twenty years. His first book, *The Fox Busters*, was published in 1978, by which time he was teaching in a village primary school. He later gave up teaching to concentrate on his writing, and has since written a great number of books for children, including *The Sheep-Pig* (winner of the *Guardian* Award), *George Speaks*, *The Hodgeheg*, *Dodos are Forever*, *The Cuckoo Child*, *Pretty Polly* and *Lady Daisy*.

Dick King-Smith is married, with three children and ten grandchildren, and lives near Bristol in Avon.

'His very name guarantee[s] quality' – *Guardian*

Amanda Harvey had two years of art training as a teenager, but left to take up several different jobs, the latest being in community mental health. It was after the birth of her first baby and wishing 'to do something different' that she took a day course for mature students at Chelsea Art School. In 1991 Amanda Harvey won the Mother Goose Award for her outstanding illustrations. She is now the mother of two children and lives with her family in Kent.

By the same author

ACE
DAGGIE DOGFOOT
DICK KING-SMITH'S COUNTRY WATCH
DICK KING-SMITH'S TOWN WATCH
DICK KING-SMITH'S WATER WATCH
DODOS ARE FOREVER
DRAGON BOY
FIND THE WHITE HORSE
HARRY'S MAD
MAGNUS POWERMOUSE
MARTIN'S MICE
NOAH'S BROTHER
PADDY'S POT OF GOLD
PETS FOR KEEPS
THE QUEEN'S NOSE
SADDLEBOTTOM
THE SHEEP-PIG
THE TOBY MAN
TUMBLEWEED
THE WATER HORSE

Dick King-Smith

The Ghost at Codlin Castle

Illustrated by Amanda Harvey

PUFFIN BOOKS

PUFFIN BOOKS

Published by the Penguin Group
Penguin Books Ltd, 27 Wrights Lane, London W8 5TZ, England
Penguin Books USA Inc., 375 Hudson Street, New York, New York 10014, USA
Penguin Books Australia Ltd, Ringwood, Victoria, Australia
Penguin Books Canada Ltd, 10 Alcorn Avenue, Toronto, Ontario, Canada M4V 3B2
Penguin Books (NZ) Ltd, 182–190 Wairau Road, Auckland 10, New Zealand

Penguin Books Ltd, Registered Offices: Harmondsworth, Middlesex, England

First published by Viking 1992
Published in Puffin Books 1994
1 3 5 7 9 10 8 6 4 2

Text copyright © Fox Busters Ltd, 1992
Illustrations copyright © Amanda Harvey, 1992
All rights reserved

The moral right of the author and illustrator has been asserted

Printed in England by Clays Ltd, St Ives plc
Filmset in Garamond

Contents

The Ghost at Codlin Castle

'Gran,' said Peter as his grandmother was tucking him up in bed, 'd'you believe in ghosts?'

'Oh yes,' said his grandmother.

'So d'you know a good ghost story to tell me?'

'Now?'

'Yes.'

'All right.'

*

Like a great many ghosts (said Gran), Sir Anthony Appleby was wary of people. It wasn't that they could do him any harm. That had been done ages ago. It was the fuss they made when they came upon him, in the winding corridors and steep stone stairways of Codlin Castle.

Some screamed and ran, some stood rooted to the spot, trembling and ashen-faced, some fainted. But no one ever said a kind word to him. In fact, no one had spoken a word of any kind to him since his death in 1588. In time past, things had not been so bad, for then the only inhabitants of Codlin Castle had been the Appleby family and their servants; all were quite used to the ghost of Sir Anthony, and though they may not have spoken to him, at least they were no trouble to him.

Nowadays things were different for the Appleby fortunes had dwindled over the centuries, until finally one of Sir Anthony's descendants had been forced to sell the family seat.

Now it was known as the Codlin Castle Hotel, where well-to-do folk came to stay, to sleep in canopied four-posters and to eat rich meals in the medieval Banqueting Hall. Sir Anthony kept bumping into them in the corridors and stairways, and all of them, it seemed, were frightened of ghosts.

'A fellow can't get any peace these days,' said Sir Anthony grumpily (like all ghosts, he talked to himself a great deal). 'One look at me and they lose their heads,' and then he allowed himself a smile, for though dressed in the costume of his age – doublet and hose, flowing cloak, high ruffed collar, sword by his side – he was, as always, carrying his head underneath one arm.

For three hundred and forty-two years he had carried it thus, ever since that fateful day when, as one of her courtiers, he had accompanied Queen Elizabeth on a visit to her fleet at Tilbury.

On the dockside there was a large puddle, and the Queen stopped before it.

'Your cloak, Sir Anthony,' she said.

Sir Anthony hesitated.

'Majesty?' he said.

'I may have the heart and stomach of a king,' said Queen Elizabeth, 'but I have the feet of a weak and feeble woman and I don't want to get them wet. Cast your cloak upon yonder puddle.'

'But Your Majesty,' said Sir Anthony Appleby, 'it is a brand-new cloak and it will get all muddy,' at which the Queen ordered that he be taken straight away to the Tower of London and there beheaded, while Sir Walter Raleigh hastily threw down his own cloak.

The years and indeed the centuries slipped by. One sultry summer's night in 1930, the stable clock was striking

twelve as the ghost made his way along a stone-flagged passageway in the West Wing, his head tucked underneath his left arm. This was how he usually carried it, to leave his sword-arm free, though sometimes he changed sides for the head was quite heavy. Once, a couple of hundred years ago, he had tried balancing it on top of his neck, just for fun, but this had not been a success. A serving-wench had come

upon him suddenly in the castle kit-
chens, making him jump so that the
head fell off and rolled along the
floor, at which the wretched girl, a
newcomer, had died of fright.

Remembering this incident as the
twelfth stroke sounded, Sir Anthony
stopped opposite a tall cheval-glass
standing in the passage, and taking

up his head with both hands, set it carefully above the great ruffed collar.

'A fine figure of a man,' he remarked to his reflection, 'though I say it myself,' and, pressing his palms against his ears to keep the head steady, he turned this way and that, the better to admire himself. He could not therefore hear the approach of soft footsteps, but suddenly saw, beside his own reflection, that of a small girl in pink pyjamas.

'Hello,' she said. 'Who are you?'

So startled was Sir Anthony that he almost dropped his head.

'My ... my name is ... is Sir Anthony Appleby,' he stammered, turning to face the child. 'And who, pray, are you, young miss?'

'I'm Biffy,' said the small girl. 'It's short for Elizabeth.'

That name again, thought Sir Anthony, but at least someone's spoken to me at last.

'Why aren't you in bed?' he said.

'Too hot,' said Biffy. 'I couldn't sleep. Why aren't you?'

'Oh, I never sleep,' said Sir Anthony. 'I'm a ghost, you see.'

'What fun,' said Biffy. 'How long have you been dead?'

'Three hundred and forty-two years.'

'Oh. So that's why you're wearing

those funny clothes.'

'Yes.'

'Why have you got your hands pressed to your ears? Have you the earache?'

'No, no,' said Sir Anthony. 'Ghosts can't feel pain. It's about the only advantage of being one.'

'Then why are you holding your head?' said Biffy.

Oh dear, thought the ghost. If I take off my head, the child will scream or faint or even die of fright. And I do so want her to say a kind word to me. One kind word and I'm sure I could rest in peace at long last, instead of having to trudge round these winding corridors and steep stone stairways for the rest of my death.

'Look,' he said. 'If I tell you a secret, will you promise faithfully not to scream or faint or die of fright?'

'I promise.'

'Well, you see, when I died, it was in a rather unusual way. I mean, it

was common enough then, but they don't do it nowadays.'

'What did they do to you?'

'They executed me. They cut off my head. That's why I'm holding it like this now. I'm just balancing it, you see. It's not attached.'

'What fun,' said Biffy. 'Take it off.'

The ghost's face wore a very worried expression.

'You promised not to scream or faint or die of fright, remember?' he said.

'Yes,' said Biffy. 'Don't worry.'

So Sir Anthony Appleby removed his head, holding it carefully by its long hair, and tucked it under his arm.

The small girl in the pink pyjamas clapped her hands in delight.

'That's wonderful!' she said, and

at these words a broad grin of pleasure spread over the bearded features.

'Oh, Sir Anthony Appleby,' said Biffy. 'You really are the nicest ghost in the whole wide world!' and because she was just the right height, she gave him a kiss on the top of his head.

Immediately the ghost of Codlin Castle vanished.

Biffy looked all round, but there was no sign of him.

She looked in the cheval-glass, but saw only her own reflection, standing there in her pink pyjamas.

So she went back to bed.

*

'Is that the end of the story?' said Peter.

'Yes, I suppose it is,' said his grandmother. 'Except that from then onward, nobody at the Codlin Castle Hotel ever saw the ghost of Sir Anthony Appleby again.'

'Because he was at peace at last, you mean?'

'Yes.'

'Because the girl said a kind word to him?'

'Yes.'

'Gran,' said Peter. 'Your name's Elizabeth, isn't it?'

'Yes. But when I was little, I was always called Biffy.'

Baldilocks
and the
Six Bears

There was once a magic forest full of fine tall trees.

In it lived not only animals, but – because it was a magic forest – fairies and pixies and elves and goblins. Some of the goblins were full of mischief and some of the elves were rather spiteful, but on the whole, the fairy people were a happy lot. All except one.

He was a hobgoblin, quite young, not bad-looking; he might even have been thought handsome except for one thing.

He hadn't a hair on his head.

Someone – probably an elf – had named him Baldilocks, and that was what everyone called him.

Baldilocks had never had a great deal of hair, and what he did have had gradually fallen out, till now he had none at all.

How sad he was. How he envied
all the other fairy people their fine
locks and tresses, each time they met,
at the full moon.

In a clearing among the trees was
a huge fairy-ring, and in the middle
of this ring sat the wisest fairy of
them all. She was known as the
Queen of the Forest.

As usual, everyone laughed when
Baldilocks came into the fairy-ring.

'Baldilocks!' someone – probably

an elf – would shout, and then the pixies would titter and the elves would snigger and the goblins would chuckle and the fairies would giggle. All except one.

She was a little red-haired fairy, not specially beautiful but with such a kindly face. She alone did not laugh at the bald hobgoblin.

One night, when everyone was teasing poor Baldilocks as usual, the Queen of the Forest called for silence. Then she said to Baldilocks, 'Would you like to grow a fine head of hair?'

'Oh, I would, Your Majesty!' cried the hobgoblin. 'But how do I go about it?'

'Ask a bear,' said the Queen of

the Forest, and not a word more would she say.

The very next morning Baldilocks set out to find a bear. It did not take him long. He came to a muddy pool, and there was a big brown bear, catching frogs.

'Excuse me,' said Baldilocks. 'Could you tell me how to grow a fine head of hair?'

The brown bear looked carefully at the hobgoblin. He knew that the only way a bald person can grow hair is by rubbing bear's grease into his scalp. But he wasn't going to say that, because he knew that the only way to get bear's grease is to kill a bear and melt him down.

He picked up a pawful of mud.

'Rub this into your scalp,' said the brown bear.

So Baldilocks took the sticky mud

and rubbed it on his head. It was full of wriggling things and it smelt horrid. But it didn't make one single hair grow.

The next bear Baldilocks met was a big black one. It was robbing a wild-bees' nest.

'Excuse me,' said Baldilocks. 'Could you tell me how to grow a fine head of hair?'

The black bear looked carefully at the hobgoblin. He too knew the only way for a bald person to grow hair. He pulled out a pawful of honey-comb.

'Rub this into your scalp,' said the black bear.

So Baldilocks took the honey and rubbed it on his head. It was horribly sticky and it had several angry bees in it that stung him. But it didn't make one single hair grow.

The third bear that Baldilocks met was a big gingery one, that was digging for grubs in a nettle patch.

Baldilocks asked his question

again, and the ginger bear, after look-
ing carefully at him, pulled up a
pawful of nettles and said, 'Rub these
into your scalp.'

So Baldilocks took the nettles and
rubbed them on his head. They stung
him so much that his eyes began to
water, but they didn't make one
single hair grow.

The fourth bear that Baldilocks
came across, a big chocolate-coloured
one, was digging out an ants' nest,
and by way of reply to the hobgoblin,
he handed him a pawful of earth that
was full of ants.

When Baldilocks rubbed it on his
head, the ants bit him so hard that
the tears rolled down his face, but
they didn't make one single hair grow.
Baldilocks found the fifth bear by the
side of a river that ran through the
forest. It was a big old grey bear, and

it was eating some fish that had been
left high and dry on the bank by a
flood. They looked to have been dead
for a long time, and when Baldilocks's
question had been asked and answered, and he had rubbed the rotten
fish on his head, they made it smell
perfectly awful. But, once again, they
didn't make one single hair grow.

Baldilocks had just about had enough. What with the mud and the honey and all the stings and bites and the stink of the fish, he almost began to hope that he wouldn't meet another bear. But he did.

It was a baby bear, a little golden one, and it was sitting in the sun doing nothing.

'Excuse me,' said Baldilocks. 'Could you tell me how to grow a fine head of hair?'

The baby bear looked fearfully at the hobgoblin. He knew, although he was so young, that the only way for a bald person to grow hair is by rubbing bear's grease into his scalp. And he knew, although he was so young, that the only way to get bear's grease is to kill a bear and melt him down.

He did not answer, so Baldilocks, to

encourage him, said, 'I expect you'll tell me to rub something into my scalp.'

'Yes,' said the baby bear in a small voice.

'What?'

'Bear's grease,' said the baby bear in a small voice.

'Bear's grease?' said Baldilocks. 'How do I get hold of that?'

'You have to kill a bear,' said the baby bear in a whisper, 'and melt him down.'

'Oh!' said Baldilocks. 'Oh no!' he said.

When next the fairy people met, and the hobgoblin came into the fairy-ring, someone – probably an elf – shouted 'Baldilocks!' and everyone laughed, except the little red-haired fairy.

The Queen of the Forest called for silence. Then she said to Baldilocks, 'You haven't grown any hair. Didn't you ask a bear?'

'I asked six, Your Majesty,' said Baldilocks, 'before I found out that what I need is bear's grease, and to get that I would have to kill a bear and melt him down.'

'That might be difficult,' said the Queen of the Forest, 'but perhaps you could kill a little one?'

She smiled as she spoke, because she knew, being the wisest fairy of them all, that high in a nearby tree a small golden bear sat listening anxiously.

'I couldn't do such a thing,' said Baldilocks. 'I'd sooner stay bald and unhappy.'

Up in the tree, the baby bear hugged himself silently.

After the others had gone away, Baldilocks still sat alone in the fairy-ring. At least he thought he was alone, till he looked round and saw that the little red-haired fairy with the kindly face was still sitting there too.

'I think,' she said, 'that bald people are much the nicest.'

'You do?' said Baldilocks.

'Yes. So you mustn't be unhappy any more. If you are, you will make me very sad.'

Baldilocks looked at her, and to his eyes it seemed that she didn't simply have a kindly face, she was beautiful.

He smiled the happiest of smiles.

'You mustn't be sad,' he said. 'That's something I couldn't bear.'

The Alien at 7B

At first sight the Alien looked like a sausage, an uncooked sausage. It was pinkish, its skin was shiny, and, like a sausage, it seemed long and thick and fat, all at the same time.

There were differences however.

To begin with, it was the size of a very large pig (if you can imagine a legless, earless pig), and then again, unlike any sausage, it had a pair of small round eyes and, between them, a mouth shaped like the opening of a letter-box. What's more, the Alien had a second pair of eyes and a second mouth at the other end of its body, so that there was no knowing which was its front and which was its rear.

It lay, motionless, on the lawn in the small front garden of 7B, Marine View, Littleton-on-Sea.

Though the round eyes and the oblong slits were open, the creature was so still that a cheeky sparrow hopped up to one of the letter-box mouths and, cocking his head on one side, peered in.

Suddenly there was a sound like a sharply indrawn breath, and the bird was sucked from sight. A slight tremor rippled down the body of the Alien, and then, after a moment, a little cloud of feathers blew out of the other mouth.

For a while, nothing else happened. It was early in the morning and few people were about yet in the little seaside town. The curtains of

the houses in Marine View were still
drawn, and the only inhabitant of 7B
to be seen was a large ginger tom-
cat, which emerged from a flap in the
back door and sauntered round to
the front garden.

At sight of the Alien, he stopped
dead in his tracks, ears pricked, tail

twitching. But seeing no movement, the cat inched forward and cautiously sniffed at the side of the fat pink body. Then, curious, he moved to one end of the thing, where a few brown feathers lay on the ground.

Once again there came that sharp sucking noise, and into the expanding oblong of the letter-box slit went the cat, tail first. For a fraction of a second, his round astonished face

looked its last upon the world, and then he was gone. Once more a ripple ran along the great sausage shape, and then the mouth at the other end blew out a little parcel of ginger fur.

Further up Marine View, the chinking of bottles told that the milkman was on his way, and before long he opened the wrought-iron gate of 7B and came in with three pints of

Gold Top. He had placed them on the highest step outside the front door and turned away before he noticed the strange object lying on the lawn, feathers at one end of it, fur at the other.

'People chuck their rubbish anywhere nowadays,' said the milkman, who was rather short-sighted, and he shut the gate and climbed back into his electric cart.

No sooner had he gone than the Alien moved.

To anyone watching, it would have seemed a mystery how the sausage shape could slowly slide along the ground without any legs. In fact, it was simply done. It merely sucked in air through one mouth and blew it out through the other. By this process, it had jetted the many millions of miles from its native planet to land, quite by chance, in Littleton-on-Sea.

Now it slid forward to the steps of 7B, its leading pair of eyes fixed upon the milk bottles.

'Schloop!' and one pint vanished

into the mouth-slit.

'Schloop! Schloop!' and the others followed.

Silently the Alien slid back to its original position. Deep within the shiny pink body could be heard a tiny tinkling noise, and then from the rear mouth came a little shower of broken glass and three gold bottle-tops.

At that moment the front door of

7B half opened, and a man in dressing-gown and slippers peered round it, yawning and rubbing his eyes.

Automatically he bent to pick up the milk bottles before he realized there were none.

'The milkman hasn't been,' he called to someone inside the house.

'Yes, he has,' a woman's voice replied. 'I heard him.'

'Well, there's no milk on the door-step.'

'Nip down the road and catch him then. He can't be far off.'

'I'm not going out in my dressing-gown and slippers.'

'Oh, all right, I'll send Debbie then,' the woman said. 'Debbie!'

'Yes, Mum?' said a girl's voice.

'Are you dressed?'

'Yes, Mum.'

'Pop down the road, there's a good girl, and get three pints. The milkman's forgotten us.'

'OK, Mum.'

The moment Debbie came out through the front door of 7B, she saw the Alien. Not that either of her parents could have failed to see it, had they come out into the garden. It was too big and strange-looking for anyone but a short-sighted milkman to miss. But they would have had no idea what it was. Debbie knew immediately.

Not for nothing had she read every science-fiction book she could lay her hands on, watched every cartoon, seen every film about creatures from outer space. There was nothing she didn't know about Aliens, and this was one, beyond the shadow of a doubt!

But was it friendly?

Keeping well away from it, in case it wasn't, she said in the politest of tones, 'Welcome to our planet.'

The Alien stared unblinkingly at her with its round eyes, but no sound came from the oblong mouth-slit.

'Look,' said Debbie. 'I've just got to fetch some milk. Don't go away.'

She went out of the gate, and, turning for another look, could see that on the other end of the great pink sausage-shaped body was a second pair of eyes and a second mouth.

Maybe I was talking to the wrong end, she thought, so she repeated her greeting, but again there was no reply.

When Debbie came hurrying back with three more bottles of milk, she was in such a rush to hand them over and return to examine the Alien more closely that she forgot to shut the front gate.

This was the opportunity for which 7A's dog had been waiting.

Every day 7B's ginger tom would sit on the dividing wall and make catty remarks, and every day the dog, a fat, bad-tempered terrier with a brass-studded collar, would hope against hope that some time or other the gate of 7B would be left open.

Then, with luck, he would catch that cat unawares and make mincemeat of him.

Now, when the dog dashed in, there was no ginger tom to be seen, but only a strange thing that looked like a giant pink sausage. The terrier

advanced upon it, barking and growl-
ing.

Debbie came back out of the front
door just in time to hear the barking
drowned by that dreadful schlooping
noise, and to see the wretched dog
disappear head first into the Alien.

Again the bloated body shuddered
a little, and then from the other
mouth a brass-studded collar came
flying out.

'This Alien,' said Debbie, 'is defi-
nitely not friendly,' and even as she
spoke, she saw it begin to slide across
the grass towards her.

She dashed inside 7B and slammed
the door.

'Debbie,' said her mother as the
family sat at breakfast. 'Why are you
gobbling your food like that?'

'It's Saturday, you know,' said her

father from behind his newspaper. 'No school today. What's the hurry?'

'There's an Alien in the front garden,' said Debbie.

'E.T. I suppose,' said her father.

'No,' said Debbie. 'This is an unfriendly Alien.'

'I expect it'll wait for you,' her mother said. 'No need to bolt your food.'

It'll wait for me all right, thought Debbie, and it'll bolt me if I'm not mistaken. And Mum. And Dad. And probably everyone in Littleton-on-Sea. I must deal with it. But how?

Let's see – it sucks things in one end and blows things out the other. Of course! That's how it propels itself, that's how it got here from outer space. I've got to persuade it to take off again before it does any more damage. But how?

It was while Debbie was washing up – one of her jobs on a Saturday – that the answer came to her. Because she was thinking hard about how to deal with the Alien, she absent-mindedly squirted much too much washing-up liquid into the bowl and it rose up in a cloud of soap bubbles.

That's it, thought Debbie! Fill the Alien full of that stuff, and it'll float away, like it or not.

Quickly she finished the breakfast things, and took a new jumbo-sized container of washing-up liquid from the kitchen cupboard.

Stealthily she made her way to the front door and peeped out through the flap of the letter-box.

To her surprise, she could see nothing.

Then all of a sudden the horrid truth burst upon Debbie. Outside, the Alien had one of its mouths, a mouth shaped exactly like the opening of a letter-box, pressed against the one in the front door of 7B!

Quick as a flash, Debbie thrust the nozzle of the washing-up container into the flap, and as she did so, she heard that dreadful schlooping noise and felt a terrible suction pull her flat against the door. For a moment she struggled madly, face pressed to the wood, feet kicking helplessly, and then it was over and she was standing in the hall, holding a jumbo-sized container of washing-up liquid that contained nothing. It was empty, sucked dry.

By the time Debbie had nerved herself to open the front door, the Alien was already airborne.

Pink, pig-sized, sausage-shaped, its skin now shinier than ever, blown tight by the pressure of the expanding liquid within its body, it gained height gradually, driven first one way, then another, as from either mouth came spasmodic bursts of soapy bubbles, while its two pairs of round eyes seemed ready to burst.

Up above 7B it rose, up above Marine View, up above Littleton-on-Sea, until at last it was lost from sight among the clouds.

Carefully Debbie set about tidying up the front garden. Thoughtfully she picked up some feathers, a parcel of what looked like ginger fur, a lot of broken glass, three gold bottle-tops, and a brass-studded collar, and

put them in the dustbin. Then she dropped the empty washing-up liquid container in as well. Then she went in-doors.

'Mum! Dad!' she said. 'It's all right now. The Alien's gone.'

'You and your Aliens!' her father said.

Her mother poured some milk into a saucer.

'Debbie, I do wish you'd stop imagining things,' she said. 'Here, take this out for the cat.'

The Adorable Snowman

In a snow-cave, half-way up Mount Everest, sat a family of yetis. There were three of them, father, mother and son, all covered in long, reddish hair.

Daddyeti was much taller than a man.

Mummyeti was the same size as a man.

Babyeti was very young, only about six months old, in fact, but still he was as big as the average six-year-old boy. But unlike the average six-year-old boy, Babyeti had never met any other living creature but Daddyeti and Mummyeti. Except for a few birds, that is. Otherwise nobody had disturbed the peace of Mount Everest during that first half year of his life.

However, that morning Babyeti got a big surprise.

'Can I go out and play, Mum?' he asked.

'All right,' said Mummyeti, 'but watch out for avalanches.'

'And don't go falling down any crevasses,' said Daddyeti.

But Babyeti had gone only a few yards from the mouth of the cave when he saw, far below, a line of little figures showing up blackly against the dazzling whiteness of the snow.

'Mum! Dad!' he called, and when his parents came out to see what was the matter, he pointed down to the distant figures.

'Whatever are those?' he said.

Daddyeti gave a grunt of annoyance.

'Humans!' he said angrily.

Mummyeti sighed.

'What a nuisance,' she said. 'Why can't they stay where they belong?'

'We haven't had any for nearly a year,' said Daddyeti.

'But what are humans, Dad?' asked Babyeti.

'Well,' said Daddyeti, 'I suppose they are a sort of monkey, except that they don't seem to have any hair on their bodies. They have to wrap themselves in all kinds of stuff to keep warm.'

'But what do they look like?'

'You can't see,' said Mummyeti. 'As well as covering up their bodies and their paws and their heads, they wear round black things they call goggles over their eyes, so that you

can't see their faces. And they're all
tied to one another with long ropes.'

'But why do these humans come
up the mountain?' asked Babyeti.

'To get to the top,' said Daddyeti.

'And do they?'

'Usually. They never did when I was a young yeti, but nowadays they almost always do.'

'And when they've got to the top, what do they do then?'

'Come down again.'

'Oh,' said Babyeti, 'I see . . . d'you think that I could meet one?'

'Certainly not!' said Mummyeti sharply.

'Why not?'

'Because humans have absolutely no respect for yetis. D'you know what they call us? They call us Abominable Snowmen.'

'You mean they'd call Dad an Abominable Snowman?'

'Yes.'

'So you'd be an Abominable Snow-woman?'

'Well, yes, I suppose so.'

'And I'd be an Abominable

Snowbaby?'

'Yes.'

'What does "abominable" mean?'

'It means detestable,' growled Daddyeti.

'And what does that mean?'

'It means hateful,' said Mummyeti. 'Though why they should hate us, I don't know. We've never done them any harm. Nor has any other yeti.'

'Yet,' said Daddyeti darkly. 'Now

then, inside the cave, both of you, and we'll block up the mouth with snow. Those humans will be up this high by nightfall.'

'Do they stop at night?' said Babyeti.

'Yes. They're frightened of the dark, I think. They get inside little shelters called tents and wait for day-light.'

Babyeti couldn't get to sleep that night. He lay thinking about the

strange humans and wondering why
they thought that yetis were hateful.
I wish I could ask one, he thought.

He lay listening to his parents snoring.

I *will* ask one, he thought sleepily.
I can quickly nip along the mountain-
side and find a human and ask it,
and then be back here before Mum
and Dad notice anything. So very
quietly he burrowed a hole through
the snow that was blocking the cave-
mouth.

The night was quite a still one, and the moon shone brightly on Mount Everest. Babyeti could see, not far below, a number of strange shapes on the steep slope, the tents of which Dad had spoken.

Swiftly and silently Babyeti scrambled down to the nearest one and, cautiously raising the flap, found himself staring at a sleeping human. Its body and its paws and its head were wrapped up, but it wasn't tied to anyone and it didn't have any goggles over its eyes. In fact, it suddenly opened them and stared back at Babyeti.

Then the human gave a gasp of surprise.

'Heavens above!' it said softly. 'The Abominable Snowman!'

'Why do you call me that?' said Babyeti. 'Abominable means detestable and detestable means hateful. What reason have you to hate me?'

'No reason at all, now I come to think of it,' said the human.

'It'd be different,' said Babyeti, 'if I were to do you any harm. But I wouldn't dream of such a thing, and nor would any other yeti. I must say, I think it's a bit unfair to call us abominable.'

'You are absolutely right,' said the human. 'I do apologize. No one could possibly hate you. In fact, I think you're a perfectly lovely little chap.'

'Oh thanks,' said Babyeti.

'What you need,' said the human, 'is a new name. I shall call you the Adorable Snowman.'

'Oh good,' said Babyeti, and he let down the flap of the tent and made his way back to the snow-cave.

When the climbers woke next morning, one of them said to the others, 'I saw a yeti last night. It came to my tent. It spoke to me. It was a perfectly lovely little chap.'

The others looked at one another.

'You've been dreaming,' they said.

When the yetis woke next morning, Babyeti said to his parents, 'I saw a human last night. I went to its tent. I spoke to it. It said I was an Adorable Snowman.'

Daddyeti and Mummyeti looked

at one another.

'You've been dreaming,' they said.

'I haven't. It's true.'

'Now, now,' they said. 'You mustn't tell lies.'

Babyeti grinned.

As if I would, he thought. What an abominable thing to say.

The Message

'Look!' said Robert to his cousin James. 'There's a bottle coming down!'

The two boys were leaning over the parapet of the stone bridge that spanned the river, and they watched the bottle sailing closer.

It was a clear glass one, with a cork in its neck, and as it passed directly beneath them, James said, 'It's got something in it.'

'It looks like a rolled-up piece of paper,' said Robert.

'A message!' said James.

'Let's get it!' they cried, and they ran off the bridge and down on to the river bank.

The current was sluggish, and the boys had no difficulty in keeping pace with the floating bottle, but it stayed stubbornly out in midstream.

'Let's not bother,' said James, who was a nervous boy by nature and, though he had learned to swim, was still scared of water. 'Let's just leave it.'

Robert, on the other hand, was a bold boy, afraid of nothing.

'Wait a bit,' he said. 'We've got to find out if that is a message inside, and if so, what it says. Maybe some-one needs help.'

Just then a motor cruiser came chugging upriver, and after it had passed them, its wake rocked the bottle and moved it a little nearer the bank.

'That's an idea,' Robert said. 'Let's find some big stones and chuck them beyond the bottle and that'll help to wash it in close enough for us to get it.'

James hesitated. I'll probably throw them the wrong side or even hit it and sink it, he thought.

'You do it,' he said. 'I'm not good at throwing like you are.'

'Well, you go and find a long stick or a branch or something,' said Robert. 'Something to hook it out with when I've got it near enough.'

Just so long as he doesn't want me to go in and get that bottle out, said James to himself as he trudged off. That river looks awfully deep. And cold. And brown and mucky. But then he's sure to want to get it out himself, Robert is. I wish I was brave like him.

By the time he got back, carrying a longish branch that he had found, Robert's accurate stone-throwing had brought the bottle much closer to the bank. Better still, it was now lodged in a clump of reeds that stopped it floating on downriver.

'See if you can reach it with this branch,' said James, but it was still too far out.

'I'm going in after it,' Robert said.

'It's too deep,' said James. 'The water will come over the top of your wellies.'

'That's not the end of the world,' said Robert. 'If it was summertime, I'd have swum out after it, but it's a bit too chilly for that,' and he began to wade in.

'Coo, it's muddy at the bottom,'

he said, 'and smelly old mud at that.'

'Be careful, Robert,' James said anxiously. 'You might get stuck.'

'Nearly there,' said Robert, and he lunged forward and grabbed the bottle by its neck. As he did so, he sank a little so that the water filled his wellies.

'You were right, James!' he shouted, laughing. 'But anyway I got it!' and he hurled the bottle up on to the bank.

'Are you all right?' said James.

'Of course.'

'Well, come on out then.'

There was a pause and then Robert said, 'I can't.'

'Why not?'

'My boots are stuck. In the mud.'

'Kick them off.'

'I can't,' said Robert, and suddenly his voice sounded strained. 'I can't get my feet out of them.

They've gone in too far.'

To his horror, James saw that Robert was now nearly waist-deep. Even as he watched, he saw that the water was creeping up. Not only was Robert stuck in the mud, he was slowly sinking in it, and the more he struggled to free his feet, the lower he sank.

He turned a white face to his cousin on the bank.

'Help me!' he panted. 'James! Help me!'

He's going to drown, thought James. He's going to keep sinking in that horrible river mud, all soft and squelchy like quicksand, until his head goes under. It doesn't matter that he's a strong swimmer, his feet are stuck inside his boots and he can't get them out. And if I go in to try to rescue him, I shall drown too. I'm not even a strong swimmer. Oh, what shall I do?

Afterwards, James never understood how it was that he answered this last question in the way that he did.

Every bit of him said 'Don't go! One drowned is bad enough, why make it two?' and yet the next thing

he knew was that he had kicked off
his wellies and belly-flopped into the

cold, cold water, and was swimming
with the mad, panicky breast-stroke
that was all he could manage.

Afterwards, he couldn't think how
he had found the strength to keep
himself afloat and somehow, Heaven
only knows how, to pull Robert free
from his trapped boots. The distance
back to the safety of dry land was no

more than a few yards, but later it seemed to James like it had been miles, before at last they sat side by side on the bank, exhausted, soaked, and shivering with cold.

Then Robert said slowly, 'You saved my life.'

James gave a sort of nervous giggle.

'You've lost your wellies,' he said. 'You can have one of mine if you like and we'll hop home like they do in three-legged races. Come on, we'd

better get moving.'

'And all for a stupid bottle,' said Robert as they stood up. 'Where is the thing anyway?'

They searched about and found the bottle lying in the long grass.

'Might as well see what's in it,' said Robert.

He pulled out the cork, and with a thin bit of stick, he fished the rolled-up piece of paper out through the neck.

He smoothed it out, and the two cousins each held a corner and scanned it.

Then they looked at one another, in amazement, for this is what was written on it.

Who Killed
Percy Fussell?

It all began when Mr Bishop dug the goldfish pool.

Up till then, everything in the garden had been lovely, and Mr and Mrs Bishop's collection of gnomes had been one big happy family.

There were five of them, grey-beards all, dressed in brightly coloured smocks and baggy trousers, with floppy caps on their heads and long pointed shoes on their feet.

Mr Bishop liked to go down to the pub of an evening for a glass of beer and a game of dominoes with his cronies, and he had named his gnomes after some of those friends.

There was Bill Stubbs (who

smoked a pipe, just like the real-life
Bill), and Harry Pickett, and Tom
Parsons, and Bob Button who walked
with a stick as the other Bob did, and
Arthur Prendergast.

Mr and Mrs Bishop were very
fond of them all. Each evening, when
Mr Bishop had finished his gardening
and was having a drink with the real
Bill and Harry and Tom and Bob
and Arthur, Mrs Bishop would come

out with a sponge and warm water and detergent, and clean up their namesakes.

Not that the gnomes got very dirty, for of course every time it rained, they had a shower. But quite often birds would perch upon them and weren't too particular what they did. Then Mrs Bishop would go into action, so that when Mr Bishop came home from the pub, all the gnomes were spick and span, each with a permanent broad smile upon his bearded features. There followed a last walk round the garden and a final 'Good-night' to Bill and Harry and Tom and Bob and Arthur, and then Mr and Mrs Bishop would go indoors for cocoa and biscuits and bed. Little did they dream what happened later in the darkness.

How many of you, I wonder, have

ever realized that when night falls, every garden gnome in the land comes to life?

Down from their little pedestals would step the Bishops' five old fellows and stretch and yawn and turn their heads this way and that to ease the stiffness caused by standing still all day. Bill Stubbs would light his pipe, and then he and Harry and Tom and Bob, leaning on his walking-stick, and Arthur Prendergast would take a

stroll around the garden, chatting happily about the day's events.

What a pleasant life they led, until
Mr Bishop dug the goldfish pool.

It was something that Mrs Bishop
had long wanted.

'It needn't be a big one,' she said
to her husband. 'You could easily dig

a hole down in the bottom corner by the privet hedge, and you could put one of those plastic liners in it, and we could have water-lilies too, and half a dozen fish or so. We could get everything down at the Garden Centre.'

None of that would have mattered to the gnomes – indeed, it could have been very pleasant for them to sit around the pool on warm nights and dabble their long pointed shoes in the water – if only Mr Bishop had not bought something else at the Garden Centre.

'Oh look!' said Mrs Bishop, as they were leaving it. 'Isn't he lovely!'

Mr Bishop looked and saw that she was pointing at another garden gnome. He was quite a bit bigger than their five, and he was seated cross-legged on a large orange toadstool with white spots. In his hands he held a long fishing-rod with a length of real line attached to it and a real wooden red-and-blue float.

'Can't you just see him, sitting by the edge of the pool with his little

float in the water?' said Mrs Bishop. 'Wouldn't he look nice!'

'I reckon he would,' said Mr Bishop.

So they bought him.

By the end of the day, everything was completed. The liner was fitted in the hole, the water-lilies in their containers placed on the bottom, the pool filled, the goldfish put in.

Finally, while Mrs Bishop stood by, wreathed in smiles, Mr Bishop set the toadstool that bore the large angling gnome beside the rim. The fishing-rod stuck out over the water, the line hung down, the float floated.

'What shall we call him?' said Mrs Bishop.

Mr Bishop looked at the face of the angling gnome. It wore a smug, self-satisfied expression.

'Reminds me of a chap I used to know called Percy Fussell,' he said. 'Ever so keen on fishing, he was, and always boasting about the size of the fish he caught. Proper loud-mouthed bighead, and grumpy with it, though I shouldn't speak ill of the dead. Fell in the river one day and drowned, Percy did. We'll call him Percy Fussell.'

'Should we?' said Mrs Bishop. 'He might fall in the goldfish pool.'

'Well, if he did, he couldn't drown, could he?' said Mr Bishop, and they laughed and said 'Good-night' to Percy Fussell and went indoors.

After dark the five resident gnomes came to life as usual and set out for their walk round the garden. On the previous night, they had come upon the hole dug in the bottom corner by the privet hedge, and wondered what it was for. Now, to their amazement, they could clearly see (for the moon was bright) a goldfish pool. And sitting beside it on a large orange

toadstool with white spots was a very big gnome, holding something in this hands.

Bill Stubbs took his pipe out of his mouth.

'Who's he?' he said.

'Never seen him before,' said Harry Pickett.

'Big chap, isn't he?' said Tom Parsons.

Bob Button pointed with his

walking-stick.

'He's fishing,' he said.

Arthur Prendergast approached the fishing gnome.

'Good evening,' he said politely.

The newcomer spun round on his toadstool.

'Can't you keep your voices down?' he hissed. 'How's a chap expected to catch fish when you lot are making all that row? If it hadn't been for you, I'd have landed one by now, or my name's not Percy Fussell. Why don't you push off?'

If that had been an isolated outburst, things might still have been all right. But it wasn't.

Every time that the Bishops' five gnomes strolled down to the goldfish pool, the smoke from Bill Stubbs's pipe curling in the night air while Bob Button's stick tap-tapped on the path, Percy Fussell would have something unpleasant to say.

At first he only told them to be quiet, but as time passed, he became ruder and ruder, until one night he rounded on them and said in a very angry voice, 'Now listen, you lot. I'm warning you. This is *my* goldfish pool, so in future you just keep away

from it or there'll be trouble, under-
stand?' and he waved his rod at them
in a threatening manner.

'Blooming cheek!' said Arthur
Prendergast as they retreated to the
upper end of the garden.

'Nasty piece of work, that Percy
Fussell,' said Bob Button, gripping
his walking-stick angrily.

'Why shouldn't we go to the
pool?' said Tom Parsons.

'We could if only he wasn't there,'
said Harry Pickett.

Bill Stubbs puffed his pipe.

'If only he wasn't there,' he repeated thoughtfully. 'Now listen to
me, lads . . .'

So it was that on the following night,
a dark and windy one, five shadowy
shapes silently approached the goldfish pool. Bill's pipe was not lit, and

Bob leaned on Arthur Prendergast's shoulder, his walking-stick under his arm so as to make no noise.

Percy Fussell sat fishing, the usual smug, self-satisfied look on his face,

when suddenly there was a rush, and a cry, and a great splash, and then silence. A ring of ripples spread from the centre of the pool, and for a little while, a string of bubbles rose up through the water and burst. Then the surface was still once more.

'Look at this!' called Mr Bishop to his wife next morning, and they stood and stared into the goldfish pool. There at the bottom lay Percy Fussell, still seated on his toadstool, his rod still in his hands, the line leading upwards, the red-and-blue float bobbing on the surface.

'However did that happen?' asked Mrs Bishop.

Mr Bishop fished the gnome out and set him once more on the brink.

'Don't know,' he said. 'Just like the real Percy Fussell. Except that this time there's no harm done.'

Sure enough, the following night, when Bill Stubbs and Harry Pickett and Tom Parsons and Bob Button and Arthur Prendergast strolled down to the goldfish pool, there was Percy Fussell, sitting on his toadstool, fishing as before. Still as stone he sat, but for all time now, and never a word he spoke nor ever would again.

As for Bill and Harry and Tom and Bob and Arthur, they dabbled their long pointed shoes in the water and smiled happily at one another, confident that no one would ever know who killed Percy Fussell.